REBOUND LOVE

Book 2

"Samantha's LOVE & ROMANCE"™ Series

By

Denise Daniella Darcy

Published by

Durango Publishing Corp.®

© 2014 Durango Publishing Corp.®

Book 2 in Durango's acclaimed "Samantha's LOVE & ROMANCE"™ Series.

Published by: Durango Publishing Corp.®

Written by: Denise Daniella Darcy

www.DurangoPublishing.com

Email: books@DurangoPublishing.com

Acclaim for Denise Daniella Darcy and *REBOUND LOVE*

"I really liked Denise's 'First Love', and now I think I like the second in her Romance Series, "Rebound Love" even more. Talk about a great plot. Sam (the heroine) goes through dangerous times, including physical earthquakes and similar in the personal relationships area." -- Pamela Sanchez, Tucson, AZ

"In the first book in the Series, First Love, the heroine Samantha has a lot of problems, but manages through her ingenuity—and a lotta luck—to get through them. In Rebound Love, she faces even bigger problems, including earthquakes and problems with her new boyfriend... The quality of the writing in both these novels is very good. In fact, it reminds me a lot of Catherine Bybee, one of my favorites. It is written at an adult level, but clearly enough that even young or new adults can really get into it. And Denise's characters are very real, and I found myself rooting for, or booing against, them." -- Ingrid Tannin, Copenhagen Denmark

"Like the first novel, First Love, Rebound Love follows the adventures, and mis-adventures, of Samantha Morgan. She has a knack of getting into precarious (and

for the reader, interesting) problems,... Whatever the situation, the plot is well written, and whether read by late teens or more mature females, it will get their attention with its attention to details, realistic developments, and lots of very interesting dialog between characters." -- Elizabeth Dubronsky, Chicago, IL

"Like most of my friends, I enjoy a good Romance novel. It's nice to curl up on an evening with some popcorn and a good book. Something like Rebound Love, a novel in the Romance & Love Series. Written by Denise Darcy, it's the second in the series of 4. It's based on the lead character, one Samantha, also known as Sam, who gets herself into one tight scrape after another. The writing is fresh, engages the reader, and before long you are actually seeing problems through Sam's eyes." -- Madelaine Crosby-Hutton, Portland, OR

"I have read maybe one-third of the second book in the Series, Rebound Love. The first novel, sorta appropriately named First Love, was a dandy. Action, problems galore, interesting characters, and a believable plot. I'm finding the same smooth writing in the current book." -- Melody Johnston, Los Angeles, CA

Also by Denise Daniella Darcy

First Love – Book 1

Rebound Love – Book 2

Cowboy Love – Book 3

Casual Love – Book 4

Available at:

www.DurangoPublishing.com

www.DeniseDaniellaDarcy.com

www.amazon.com/Rebound-Love-Samanthas-Romance-romance-ebook/dp/B00OBJ46QU/

FREE BONUS – ALTERNATE ENDINGS

Hi Readers, Denise here. I just wanted to let you know that I have an unexpected bonus for you. I have written 2 alternate endings for *REBOUND LOVE,* and they are yours free.

Why, you may ask? Simple. I always strive to give more than the anticipated, more than the normal. Both endings dramatically change the outcome and are real page-turners.

Get your FREE copy now at:

http://www.denisedanielladarcy.com/ reboundlovealternateendings

Just my way of giving you something extra and thanking you for reading my books.

I am busy writing more stories about Samantha's adventures in love so check my website www.DeniseDaniellaDarcy.com for the most up-to-date list. Or just get my newsletter to stay on top of new developments at:

http://www.denisedanielladarcy.com/newsletter

Happy reading -

Denise Daniella Darcy - "Triple D to my friends"

PS. And as an added SPECIAL BONUS, at the end of this story I have attached a SNEAK PREVIEW of *COWBOY LOVE*, Book 3 in the series. Enjoy!

FYI - The stories in *Samantha's LOVE & ROMANCE Series* can be read in any order. The stories are linked but each one is a separate story. Research has shown that most readers do prefer to read them in sequence.

Other Titles By Durango Publishing Corp.®

Table of Contents

Chapter 1 -- Erotic yoga

"Now really reach into that stretch," the instructor bubbled at the front of the room. "Keep your center. Good!"

Sam felt ridiculous. She was in a room with a dozen elastic-clad women. Every one of them was on their own little plastic rug with her bottom stuck up into the air. *Is my center the place that didn't want to notice that everyone here is thinner than me? Because I think I found it.*

It wasn't that Sam was fat, there was just too much of her. She had wide hips and a round rear end and her breasts were always in the way. Even her brown hair was big. Its thick brown curls were currently falling into her eyes.

The instructor called out a new position, and Sam had no idea what it was. Every position had a ridiculous and supposedly mystical name, like Irritated Crab and Crane Shrugging. *When do we do Woman Getting Out of Here?* Isa had convinced her that tagging along to her yoga class would be good for her.

"You never do anything, you need to get out of the house more. And work doesn't count," Isabel had said.

"I don't want to get out of the house. The house is where my cat and pajamas and the internet all are. I've never been a joiner and it never bugged you before." She and Isa had already had variations on this conversation at least a billion times and she had known where it was going. She hated where it was going.

"It's not good for you now that Aiden's gone." Isa had put on her mom voice. Sam groaned. "If you just stew alone you'll never move on." And eventually, Sam had grudgingly agreed to accompany Isa today.

She scrambled to copy what the incredibly flexible stranger in front of her was doing. She tried not to give Isa a dirty look, as her friend stretched and contorted lithely at her side. Normally Sam didn't mind that Isa was everything she wanted to be: Outgoing, thin, athletic, and blonde. Today it pricked at her insecurities and made her more irritated.

Maybe I don't want to get over him. She arched her back in an approximation of the proper motion. The last time she and Aiden had been together, he'd bent her backwards and kissed her all over, from her navel to her throat. She remembered how his fingertips had traced up and down her spine. The feeling was delicious and it made her shiver. His tanned hands stood out against her ivory skin as he massaged and teased her. He knew all her most sensitive secret places. He kissed her nipples, and they crinkled under his soft, smooth lips. He nibbled the lobes of her ears, his breath soft and his cheek pressed to her cheek. Then he had kissed her deep and with passion. When he released her mouth her lips had been throbbing and she felt a flush in her cheeks.

Remembering, Sam's body relaxed and she threw herself into the stretch. She imagined Aiden's hungry hands and mouth and shut her eyes. "Mmmmm..." she breathed.

When he rolled over and placed her on top of him she'd straddled him and eased herself onto his shaft. With her flesh enveloping his and her arms behind her head she rode him. Her hips rocked slowly at first, gently provoking moans from his lips, and stoking the pulsing heat inside her. As her pleasure grew, she pushed harder, and he met her thrust for thrust. As they moved together she could feel him slipping in and out of her slick tightness. He reached up and stroked her, then pinched her sensitive nipple in his fingers. She gasped and her rhythm increased, the needy edge of her passion coming to the forefront. She ground him into her, and he pounded back. "Oh, god, Aiden," she whispered on shallow breath, "I'm coming!"

Her pleasure shot through her with blistering intensity. Her muscles contracted around him sending another wave of sensation through her. She was still feeling little waves and tremors as Aiden flipped her over and topped her. Sensitive as she was now, his swift thrusts drove her back over the edge. She bit her lip and her breath came in ragged gasps as she exploded again. Aiden groaned and came with her, his body shaking with the violence of the pleasure he took from her. They'd fallen asleep later, still naked, with their legs tangled together, clinging to each other like survivors of a shipwreck embrace a life ring.

As the memory faded, Sam realized that the class had gone entirely silent. She opened her eyes to see every eye in the room on her. The instructor had gone pale and her mouth was wide open. To her horror, she wasn't even doing one of the yoga stretches anymore. No, she was flat on her back, knees bent, legs open. *Oh my god. What was I doing?* She thought hard and realized she had been speaking out loud. *I said I was coming. I was moaning. Oh no! Please tell me I wasn't humping thin air.* She groaned.

Beside Sam, Isa had her hands over her mouth trying to hold in her laughter even as her eyes tried to convey sympathy and concern. The other students looked baffled for a moment. Then, rippling from one end of the room to the other the giggles started.

The instructor coughed and managed to squeak, "I think class is over for today. Good, uuuh, good job everyone."

Sam had to withstand the looks and whispers of all the cute little yoga girls in the locker room as she threw her jeans and sweatshirt back on. Isa, who was the type of person who wore yoga pants everywhere just because, was waiting for her at the front doors. When they got into Isa's car, she threw her arms around Sam. "Girlfriend, we have got to get that imagination of yours under control."

Sam squeezed her eyes shut and stared at the ceiling of the Hyundai. "How bad was it?"

Isa squeezed her hand. "It was pretty bad. You don't want the gory details. You want to watch enough reality TV to cause brain damage so you can forget this ever happened."

Sam gave her friend a sick grin. "Forget what ever happened?"

"That's the spirit!"

But I'm much better at dwelling and obsessing than forgetting, Sam thought, as she tried to shower off her feelings. Intense, lingering embarrassment mingled with the depression and regret she'd been carrying already. She cried a little, in the tired way of someone who has cried much more than they ought to already.

Aiden had had to go back to his hometown on the West Coast, almost exactly as far from Buffalo and Sam as possible without leaving the country. She couldn't blame him, his mother was very ill and needed constant care from someone responsible. Aiden's overprotective streak had developed as a reaction to the deadbeat nature of the rest of his family, so the woman had nobody else to turn to.

It's still completely unfair, though.

Sam couldn't leave her job. Uncle Ty relied on her, but more than that her work was important to her self-respect. She didn't have much to be proud of except how she'd built herself up from a humble coffee girl to junior partner. The thought of not being that any more terrified her to the core.

Neither of them had been worried about the distance, at first.

Sam had blithely assumed that the difficulties of a long distance relationship would be nothing compared to the power and brilliance of their love. *God, I was so wrong.* Even though Sam could afford to fly out to see him nearly once a week their relationship had crumbled before her eyes.

She couldn't understand the pressure he was under as the full time caregiver to a proud woman. From across the continent she couldn't even lend a helping hand. As she felt him pull away from her, her faith in him had shattered. He could see it happening but was powerless to reassure her.

He didn't deserve her insecurity and doubt, she knew, and her guilt only made her defensive. *We were such a mess.*

The end had come quickly, though Sam had yet to decide if that was a good or bad thing. Only six weeks after he'd moved away, Aiden broached the idea of a breakup.

"Better to end it now, while we can still look each other in the eye and be friends," he'd offered.

There had been tears, and the worst fights of all. But eventually Sam had to give in. When Aiden knew he was right he was immovable.

But I don't have to like it.

Another two grey months had passed and springtime was chasing the snow off the

Buffalo streets, but Sam still had mixed feelings. She wanted another option to magically present itself, but every day brought more disillusionment.

Chapter 2 -- Hong Kong convention

The next morning at the offices of Morgan Advertising, Sam tried to lose herself in the endless supply of misplaced files, customer contacts, and deadlines. When Uncle Ty blew in mid-morning, she was embroiled in negotiating a new contract by e-mail and taking care of six different loose ends in the lapses between messages.

Uncle Ty dropped a plane ticket in front of her. It landed in the only six inches of bare desk there were.

She eyed it like it might turn into a snake at any moment. "No. No no no no no. This is not the best time. No. This is the worst time..." She glared up at him, suspiciously. "You always handle the conferences. Isa got to you, didn't she?"

Uncle Ty put on his innocent face, an unconvincing thing at best. He spread a hand over his heart and said, "I have no idea what you're talking about. I simply think you're ready to handle the... excitement." He shuddered. His lack of enthusiasm for industry conferences was no secret. Sam's guess was that there were not enough single and attractive ladies at them to suit her uncle, or they were there but would have the information necessary to seek revenge upon his business. Either way he tended to find six stupid yet attractive young women to take his mind off the stress once he got back.

But, though Uncle Ty was many things, petty or mean were not among them. He wasn't the type to send Sam on jobs just to avoid them himself.

If even Uncle Ty thinks I'm in a rut maybe things are worse than I want to believe. It takes a lot of concern to push through the layers of hornball.

She sighed and picked up the ticket. The plane left for Hong Kong in a week. She had to admit that the excitement of a week in such an exotic place was kind of tempting. She was still annoyed, but if she was going to be pressured to do things, this was a much better option than another bout of yoga.

The annual Advertising Innovation Convention, though practically useless was a nice feather in the company's cap. Someone had to go, and it seemed like this time it had to be Sam.

Of course, she still wasn't going down without a fight. "I'll need to put in a lot of overtime this week to get ready to be away..." The ticket was in her hand, between them. *I will be damned if I take this on just to please you.*

"Certainly." Uncle Ty's handsome face was serene.

"And the company is going to pay for my expenses while I'm there?"

"Of course. I know I only survive such things by using room service to a scandalizing degree."

"Ok. And now, this is very important so look at me." She took a deep breath, "Uncle Ty, you are absolutely forbidden to have sex on my desk while I'm gone."

He looked briefly pained, then smiled. "For you? Of course."

Sam pocketed the ticket. A convention full of strangers actually sounded like a perfect place to lose herself for a week. The panels didn't actually matter, what mattered was only that the company made an appearance, then they could put *Attended AIC* on their credentials for another year. Customers didn't know how useless it really was. She could go through the motions and then veg out in her hotel room every night, an ocean away from

Aiden and the people who wanted her to forget him.

Uncle Ty grinned. There was a bit of victory in his voice as he continued, "But I make no promises regarding chairs, walls, or other office decor."

Despite herself, Sam laughed a little and threw a file at him. "God! You're a dirty old man!"

His smile was proud, "Damn straight."

For the rest of the day Sam's general levels of irritation were a bit less. When she felt Uncle Ty's concerned gaze rest on her she remembered that Aiden wasn't the only person who's ever loved her. It didn't do much to ease the gaping hole in her heart, but for the first time in a long while she felt less like giving the world a black eye.

Isa came in to pick up their deliveries in the early afternoon. They had met because Isa was a courier for many of the businesses downtown. The first time Isa -- Isabella to Sam at the time -- had stuck around to chat, Sam had been flabbergasted. She'd assumed that the smart, beautiful girl would want nothing to do with her. Now Isa was the best friend Sam had ever had.

When Sam told her about the upcoming trip, Isa was simultaneously excited for her and concerned to have her out of sight for so long. The result was an explosion of energy. "There's so much to do! We have to get you ready!"

"I was just going to use my business suit. And wear my regular clothes during the down times..." But she saw the pleading look on Isa's face.

"Fine. But I am not spending more than two hundred dollars, total." For once she left the office at the same time as Uncle Ty, and let Isa take her shopping for things she didn't really need. *When there's only two people in the world who care,* she figured, *I suppose you'd better humor them.*

Chapter 3 -- Tom the sound guy

Sam got off the plane in Hong Kong in a blur. Her last few days in the States had been a whirlwind of last minute details.

The cat had to be taken care of, things at work needed to be squared away, and all the time there were random things she needed to remember to throw in her bags.

Normally for business trips she drove herself to the airport, or caught a cab, but this time both Isa and Uncle Ty saw her off. It was a bit draining, actually.

Isa teared up and Uncle Ty was full of last minute advice and innuendo. Though Sam was warmed by their attention, she also found it exhausting and felt a bit guilty about how glad she was to leave them behind at boarding.

She took a taxi to the hotel where the convention would be held. She intended to explore before she went home, but for the moment all she wanted was to know where her bed was and take a shower.

It had been the longest flight she'd ever been on; with a layover in Branson, Missouri of all places before flying over the seemingly infinite expanse of the Pacific Ocean. Apparently the flight had been cheap because of the insanity of the flight plan.

At the moment, the lights of the city flashed by without exciting any interest in her.

Thank goodness hotels are the same everywhere, she thought as she checked in. The lady behind the desk spoke English but even if she hadn't the basic check in procedure didn't actually require much communication.

It was 6PM here, and there were only a few events scheduled for the night. Sam's eyes flicked over the convention schedule; she had volunteered to be part of a panel on troubleshooting in a small business environment tomorrow, but tonight there wasn't much she had to do. She decided to show up to see Social Networking: Friend or Foe? but that was it.

An hour later she had settled into her room and taken a shower, deciding that for tonight she didn't care if anyone minded her jeans. Of course, she regretted that decision instantly when she walked into a conference room full of serious faced business suited professionals. *Too late now,* she sat down in the back. A couple of fresh faced people took the stage and began a staged discussion of how to use Facebook to promote your advertising business. Sam yawned.

"Riveting, eh?" a voice dripping with sarcastic laughter whispered behind her.

Without thinking about it, Sam nodded. Another yawn prevented her from replying.

A face poked over her shoulder, "Hey, hot stuff. Mind handing me that cable? It's ok, it's not live." Sam nearly fell out of her chair, her surprised squeak earning her some dirty looks from the rows ahead of her.

She turned around to see a tall, scruffy looking young man with his sleeves rolled up past his elbows. He had a tool belt slung low on his slim hips with various technical looking things poking out of the pouches, and facial hair somewhere between a five o'clock shadow and a goatee. There was a hoop in one of his bushy, dark eyebrows. He had laughing, almond shaped eyes.

While Sam gaped, the man swung himself into the seat next to her and picked the cable up himself. He seemed to be splicing it into a different one.

"You here for the duration?" he asked with a gesture that seemed to encompass the hotel and everything in it. His voice was light and somewhat gravelly, with a slight accent that put emphasis in unexpected places.

Sam ventured a nod. "I- I'm here for the convention, yes." To her own ears she sounded like a scared little girl and she tried to compensate by putting on her business voice "And you are?"

He stuck out a moderately grease stained hand, "Tom Wong. Singer, songwriter, musician. And I'm your sound guy for all this," again his airy gesture took in everything about the convention. Sam put her hand in his, and he raised it to his lips. When she snatched it back he grinned and shrugged.

While talking, Tom was busy wiring two cables together with expert movements of his long fingered hands. As he wrapped electrical tape around the finished product, Sam realized she was completely ignoring what was happening onstage. *Super professional there, girl.*

"Well," Tom said, "Unfortunately I have a lot to get done tonight so I must leave you. But I would love to see *much more* of you soon." He gave her another sweeping look and a mischievous smile, then he straightened up and walked away, leaving through one of the employee doors that blend into the walls and hotel guests are not supposed to notice.

Sam blinked. Her jetlagged brain slowly adding things up. *Was that guy flirting with me?* Luckily, she was fairly familiar with the intricacies of social media because she did not hear a single word of the presentation. Afterward she meandered back to her room and, flinging herself onto the hard bed, fell into a fitful sleep.

Chapter 4 -- Mixed feelings

Uncle Ty was not a big fan of hard work, so Morgan Advertising's contributions to business conventions was always minimal. Sam's panel was a Q&A session where audience members first shared problems they'd encountered in the past and the panel members answered with how they would have handled the situation, followed by the group brainstorming the best solution from everyone's input.

Sam thought the whole thing was pretty useless. *I don't think I've ever had the same problem pop up twice, unless it's Uncle Ty's filing.* But she didn't have to prepare anything, just show up looking nice.

She slept in as late as possible and then put on her new suit. It had been one of the many things Isa had insisted she buy, so now she owned two suits.

Admit it, you're never wearing the old one again, so you still only have one suit.

The new one was much more comfortable and also a lot more attractive. It was navy blue with baby blue pinstripes. It hugged her chest and torso snugly, accentuating her waist before flaring at her hips. With a pair of comfortable heels the outfit made her feel competent and cool, instead of awkward and sad as she usually did lately.

She stepped up to the table on the stage and started to pin the little microphone to her chest. "Here, let me help you with that," Tom stepped close to her and adjusted the mic. He was close enough that she could feel his body heat, his fingers brushed against the fabric of her suit just hard enough to stimulate her skin underneath.

She looked up at him, and his eyes met hers. "So, beautiful stranger, are you going to tell me your name?"

Though he was only asking for her name, his tone was unmistakably seductive. And to her embarrassment and surprise, Sam felt herself responding to it. Heat flooded her and she felt her heart jump. She backed away hastily and tripped over a chair, landing squarely on her butt. A few people nearby tittered, but Tom just smiled and offered her his hand. *He acts like he knocks women down with a smile all the time. Cocky punk.* But she felt a jolt of excitement as his long fingers wrapped around hers and he pulled her to her feet. She stood there, unwilling to release his hand, it felt so good wrapped around hers.

He ducked his head and whispered in her ear, "Let's turn it on, hmm?"

This time he did chuckle as she jumped back, blushing furiously. He pointed to her microphone. "The switch is so small that some people can't find it. Some people even claim it doesn't exist. But," he closed the distance between them again and murmured, "I am very good." He flipped a tiny switch on the back of her mic and stepped off the stage. Sam had just enough time to scramble to her seat as the panelists were announced.

She knew her face was still a little red when the announcer called "Samantha Morgan, Morgan Advertising, USA." At the back of the room she saw Tom wave hugely and silently mouth, "Nice to meet you, Samantha!" before he slipped out the double doors.

Sam fanned her face with a blank paper as the first question was posed. *How does that guy not get fired?* she wondered. *Or arrested for sexual harassment?*

Thoughts of police led her immediately to thoughts of Aiden and the familiar gut punch sense of loss and regret. She was guiltily aware of lingering feelings of arousal and she felt like she was betraying him. *Girl, you are so screwed up.* She flopped her head into her hands and groaned.

"Miss Morgan, are you well? Do you need the first aid team?" The panel announcer, the whole table of panelists and every member of the audience was looking at her. She felt her blush spring back to life and had to choke back another groan.

"I'm fine. Just, um, jet lagged." She sipped from her water glass, wishing it wasn't clear so she could hide behind it. *This is going to be a very long hour and a half...*

By the time the event was over, Sam was mentally exhausted. Her mind kept stubbornly returning to thoughts of Aiden, her feelings of embarrassment, and worst of all the way Tom made her feel when he stood close to her. Normally she could wing a panel like this one easily. This time she had forced herself to write down each question, knowing she'd forget it before her turn to speak if she didn't. As it was she had to bite her tongue to keep from muttering things to herself. Things like "jerk," "oh my god," and "yes." She felt absolutely fried.

She took a shower and lay down naked on the bed. She wished Aiden were here with her. When she felt overwhelmed he could always make her feel better. She let her hands wander over her breasts, relaxing as she imagined him squeezing them. She imagined the taste of his mouth and the feel of his breath on her skin as he kissed her. Her nipples crinkled under her fingers and she pretended it was his mouth that electrified them.

One hand wandered lower, slipping into her womanhood. She imagined long, rough fingers gripping her thighs and probing her as she stroked herself. She teased her nipple, gasping as she pictured white teeth pinching them gently, rough facial hair brushing against her tender flesh. Simultaneously, she fondled the bud inside her cleft, trying to feel the callouses of a manly hand.

As her excitement built, each tiny motion sent bigger and bigger jolts of sensation down her legs and up her spine. She ran her fingers harder and faster through her slick folds, each time they brushed against her sensitive peak she shivered. Moaning, she arched her back, feeling her pleasure reach its breaking point. She bit her lip and cried out as her release washed over her. Throbbing heat radiated out from where her fingers played and she writhed as each wave took her.

As she lay there panting, with little tremors of passion still shooting through her, she wished she wasn't so alone. *I want those long fingers all over me for real... Wait, that's not right.* Aiden had strong, square hands. They weren't soft, but they were definitely not long and rough. And Aiden was always clean shaven. She had been imagining Tom! Embarrassment knotted her stomach and she covered her face with her hands. *What is wrong with me?*

She got off the bed, it felt like she'd cheated on Aiden there and she didn't want to look at it any more. She threw on some clean jeans and a tank top. She definitely didn't want to be in her room for a while, and if she stayed in the hotel and saw Tom? *I think I might spontaneously combust from shame if I see him right now. I need to get out of here.* She decided to go exploring. Maybe even find a present for Isa.

Chapter 5 -- EARTHQUAKE!!

Sam was in the Stanley Market, wondering if Isa would prefer a cheongsam or something more touristy as a gift. Ideally, the dress should be tailored, but Isa had a model's figure and it would probably look great on her. *But stores at home carry them too. Maybe she'd prefer some of those scary looking herbs?*

She'd wandered around for several hours. First she had drifted along with the crowd, following the smell of incense to a huge temple with giant incense burners hanging from the ceiling. After that, she hopped onto a tourist bus and got off when she saw a string of little restaurants. She found a place with a line at the door but reasonable prices and when she got a place at the bar she had some of the most delicious dim sum she'd ever tasted. She got a second order to go and then meandered over to the shopping area.

As she contemplated a tiny replica of the enormous Buddha statue that she hadn't managed to find yet, Sam felt the ground shake. *An earthquake? Cool. I never notice them when they happen. I'll have a story to tell when I get back home.*

But then the rumbling came again, stronger, and she saw a number of the shoppers around her looking concerned. Shop owners turned to each other, talking in low urgent tones.

I need to get back to the hotel, Sam decided, trying to bury her growing nervousness under specific action. As she turned toward the bus stop a roar filled her ears, rising from the ground like nothing she had ever heard before. The bucking street threw her to her hands and knees.

I've got to find somewhere safe. People were running in all directions, or trying to at least, most being tossed around every time they stood. A woman stepped right on Sam as she tried to flee and more people were headed towards her. Sam crawled to the side of the street and crouched behind a vendor's overturned table. It did her absolutely no good as the ground seemed to drop out from under everything.

Sam, the table, and thousands of strangers fell six feet, only to be tossed in the air again.

Time slowed. Sam could hear cars crashing somewhere nearby, and screams. The buildings lining the street were all swaying, their windows exploded, and raining glass on the people below. She landed hard, bounced, and hit her head on the shaking pavement. Her vision darkened and she blacked out.

When she woke up, everything around her was dark. Night had fallen and the power was out. Without the brilliant city lights, the pitch blackness was only pierced by an occasional flashlight beam. Sam checked herself, she was sore all over but nothing seemed broken.

And my head is killing me. Her phone had no signal, *big shock there,* but she used the flashlight function to pick her way through the rubble towards the nearest flashlight beam. She was still clutching the paper take-out bag, but the bottom had ripped out and it was empty. She flung it away.

It was being wielded by a man in a safety helmet. Sam had never been in a situation like this before. *I think I'm supposed to ask for help, but I don't think I really need it.* "Sir? Could you tell me which direction the Marriott is in?"

"Wait over there." His flashlight beam swept over to an emergency vehicle. A crowd of dirty, wide-eyed people crowded silently around it. Some had shock blankets wrapped around their shoulders.

"But I-"

"Over there!" he snapped. *Jeez, way to be the calm, reassuring rescuer there, dude. But I suppose we're all having a bad day.* Too dazed to argue or come up with an alternate plan, Sam joined the throng of waiting people. *I guess I'm just one more victim. Lame.*

She waited for an hour, watching as more and more people joined the silent group. Nobody spoke. Occasionally a siren and commotion would announce that another person had been found, one with severe enough injuries to need immediate removal to a hospital. Sam found herself growing irrationally jealous of them. *I am so close to just walking away from here. I think*

I could retrace my steps. But my battery is low.

Even after a blow to the head, she wasn't quite willing to trust that she could navigate a strange city in pitch blackness. *I wonder what I have to do to get one of those blankets?*

She sat down and watched through slitted eyes as another flashlight beam approached. The way the light flared she couldn't tell if the person behind it was an emergency worker or another victim come to join the herd.

Actually, it was neither. "Samantha?" Tom's voice called. The beam panned over the crowd and stopped on her face.

She flinched away, the light was blinding after so much dark. "Hey!"

"Samantha! Thank goodness! Are you hurt? I knew I'd find you." He knelt next to Sam, his brows furrowed in concern, but he had a little crooked smile, too. A familiar face, one that didn't look as lost as she felt, flooded Sam with joy. She flung her arms around him, giggling stupidly. He held her gently, petting her back and repeating, "Hey there, easy..." until she could talk again.

He pulled her up and led her away. None of the victims or emergency people said anything or tried to stop them. Hand in hand, they slowly navigated the shattered, black city. Occasionally he would pick out a shop or an alleyway with his flashlight beam and tell her a story about the place. This was the place he won his first fight. That was where he used to practice guitar. That was the bar he went to after shows; that one was completely destroyed and Tom insisted on a moment of silence for it.

Sam watched his face. *His whole home is basically gone. Sane people are in shock, or crying, or angry. How is he making jokes?*

Chapter 6 -- Together with Tom

Dawn was breaking when they finally reached the hotel. The lobby was quiet, but a number of people were asleep on the couches and chairs, and a few on the floor. They passed the sleepers silently and went up to Sam's room.

The furniture was knocked all over, and the mirror was broken, but the bed was fine and they both sat down on it. Sam had taken some Ibuprofen and used the ice pack from Tom's first aid kit as they walked, but hadn't wanted to slow down long enough to check for anything else.

Now, Tom helped her wash off the scrapes on her hands. "You really were lucky this was the worst you got." Sam nodded; she guessed there were people who had not survived, let alone with just a bump and a few scrapes. She hissed as the alcohol burned her raw palms, and he instantly stopped to stroke her cheek. "Sorry," he whispered.

Sam felt the rising excitement Tom provoked in her. She remembered the last time she'd been on this bed, when it had been Tom in her fantasy, not Aiden. And Tom had come to save her. He'd noticed she was gone before the earthquake hit, and had searched each tourist trap in turn until he found her. Her heart pounded in her chest as his enormous hands wrapped tenderly around her shoulders.

She looked into his face, eyes wide. Keeping her eyes locked on his, she laid a hand on his cheek, and trailed her thumb across his lower lip. It was warm and dry. She saw excitement light his eyes at her touch. "Tom, thank you for coming to get me." Her voice was low and husky, she hardly recognized it.

He bent his head, until his lips were just centimeters from hers. His deep breath ruffled her bangs. He must have borrowed her mouthwash because he smelled like spearmint. Then, as if reaching a decision, his arms encircled her and he kissed her. Sam marveled that a man so full of himself could be so tender. His every move was so gentle that even her aching body registered only pleasure. He helped her slowly remove her shirt, and unclasped her bra with a deft movement, freeing her full, ivory white breasts.

Sam reveled in the newness of him. After the events of the night she trusted him absolutely, but every inch of him was new and exciting. She traced his collarbone and his hard jawline, tasting his salt sweat. He took her mouth in his and he tasted sweet. His hands explored her body softly but his tongue was fierce, it blazed into her mouth ravenously.

He pulled his shirt off over his head and she was amazed again at how unfamiliar he was. His chest was sprinkled with dark hair and the muscles flexing in his abs led her eye down to his slender hips. She grabbed him by the arms and pulled him down for another lingering, searing kiss. She trembled and felt tingling excitement inside her at the apex of her legs where she could feel his hard arousal pressing against her.

Just as she'd imagined, he cupped her breast in his hand and took her hard nipple into his mouth. As he worked it with his lips and tongue she moaned and whispered his name, "Oh, Tom..." Even the name felt exotic in her mouth.

He traced down her belly with his lips, and nibbled her navel as he unbuttoned her jeans and slid them and her panties off her hips. He buried his head between her thighs and she grabbed a handful of his hair as his tongue rasped over her clit. He tasted and tortured her with his mouth, his tongue gliding between her inner lips and swirling around her bud. She was building to an intolerable pressure and she heard herself begging, "Oh please, please, please!"

But he pulled himself back before she came, looking at her panting in front of him and she knew he liked having her in his power like this.

Just like his teasing, he liked to see her hot for him. He slipped off his pants and entered her, his motion deliberate and agonizingly slow. She was teetering on the edge of ecstasy, but when she tried to raise her hips and bury him fully inside her he pressed her back down. When he finally filled her she was shaking underneath him.

Finally he released her hips and began to move inside her. Sam was half crazed from waiting and met his thrusts hungrily. She found his mouth with hers and tasted him again. She felt she could not have enough of her inside him.

As his motion intensified, she clung to him, her body throbbing. She ground her hips into him as her passion overcame her. She bucked and convulsed around him, practically sobbing out his name again. He gathered her up in his arms, pressing her to his chest as she climaxed, and his rhythm became frantic inside her. He thrust into her harder and deeper than ever and she felt his body stiffen under her hands. He groaned and as he slammed into her once more he shook violently and she felt him spill into her.

They cuddled up together. Tom insisting on being the little spoon, "I don't want to wind up choking on all your gorgeous hair in my sleep," he insisted, throwing his hands into the air to save himself from the pillow Sam tried to smack him with.

Chapter 7 -- Smile!

When Sam woke up the sky outside her window was dark. Everything inside was dark, too, *so I guess the power's still off. How long was I asleep?*

Tom was gone, but there was a note left on the pillow. Sam read it by the light of her cellphone, quickly to conserve the batteries.

Hey Babe,

If you're still tired go back to sleep, there's still no power or water. But if you're up and want to help out there's plenty to do and you improve the scenery immensely. I'll save you some of the barbecue.

Kiss,

Tom

She sat in the dark on the bed, trying to think. Part of her wanted to dash out and find Tom immediately, but there was a sinking feeling in her stomach that matched her rising anxiety. *What do I think I'm doing here anyway? Tom's practically a stranger!*

Two days ago she would have sworn she'd never sleep with anyone but Aiden again. Now she wanted to glue herself to Tom's side. *Which is stupid, because I have to go back home. We're doomed, and the more I fall for him the more it'll kill me to leave.*

On the other hand, leaving was something Sam desperately wanted to do. This place felt unsafe and she knew Uncle Ty and Isa, and probably her parents too, would be worried about her. She couldn't even call them and let them know she was OK until her phone could get a signal again.

How does an earthquake kill cell phones anyway? Don't they run off satellites or something? She wondered if the airport was running, or would be soon, and if she would be able to get a seat among the inevitable crowd of tourists fleeing for their homes.

Sam got dressed and poked her nose into the hall. She could hear the rattle of a generator somewhere nearby and a string of emergency lights cast a weak yellow light.

Out of habit she headed for the elevator, then cursed and found the stairwell. *You could have told me where to go find you, punk,* she thought, *or where to avoid you.* She had nobody else here, and he felt safe to her, but losing Aiden had been worse than anything she'd ever felt before and she never wanted to feel that kind of loss again.

So she dawdled. The hotel had taken on some people who had been displaced by the quake, but not as many as Sam would have thought. There was a generator humming on most floors and two on the ground floor where a crowd of people milled around, hoping for news. Sam joined them long enough to pick up that so far there hadn't been any word about the airport or the likelihood of phone service coming back and then moved on again.

She found Tom in the courtyard amongst what did indeed look like the aftermath of an enormous, if cheerless, cookout. Six grills were standing in a semicircle, and a lone chef was still sleepily tending one. Tom was at a folding table covered in grilled meat, stuffing portions into plastic baggies. Sam decided to pretend not to notice that his hands were grease stained again. There were hundreds of bags already full and there seemed to be enough meat to fill hundreds more.

"Hey gorgeous!" Tom called when he saw her. He dropped a kiss onto her lips. When she failed to respond he pulled back and gave her a measuring look. Sam dropped her eyes.

"Huh," he blinked and then rallied, "The cooks realized all their perishables were going to go bad with the refrigeration off. You missed out on the ice cream, but help yourself to steak. The rest we're going to send out to the emergency teams. Keeps it all from going to waste, and also will make the canned stuff last."

Sam nodded and managed to dredge up a half smile and a hoarse, "Okay." She worked in silence for a while as Tom occasionally chatted with hotel staff passing by. He seemed to know everybody

Her own silence pressed on her like a ten ton weight. "Tom?"

She had his instant attention, which only made her feel worse. His grin was warm, "What's wrong, doll?"

I usually hate baby names, why don't they bother me from him? She took a deep breath, "I think I need to explain some things to you."

He led her to the outdoor swimming pool which was cracked, empty, and deserted. It was also very dark, this far from the emergency lights. *Good, I don't want to have to see his face, or let him see me crying.*

With the light pollution from the city gone, the stars were brilliant. She stared resolutely at them as she told Tom everything. She talked about her fears over the days to come. How much her family must be worrying. And also about Aiden; meeting, loving, losing him. The months of gray after them.

As she had predicted, there were tears coursing down her face before she was done. "And I already don't want to leave you behind. And it's so confusing because I really want to get home. And don't you worry that I'm using you? We don't have any future together, maybe you don't even want one, I don't know! And I just couldn't stand going through it all, all over again." She faltered, aware that she'd been babbling.

Tom covered her hand in his. "So you're beating yourself up now to save hurting later?" He was teasing her, but his voice was soft.

Sam couldn't deny the truth in the accusation, so she stayed silent.

"One place we didn't walk past last night," he said, "Is the house I lived in as a baby. I didn't stay there long and the adoption people aren't allowed to tell me where it is so I couldn't show you. My parents were into drugs or something. I just remember bits and pieces. The couch was blue. There was a dog but it wouldn't let me pet it. And I remember gun shots and a scream. The adoption people came and took me out of there. I think my birth parents are probably dead now, or in jail."

He settled back on his elbows, and stretched his long legs out in front of him, still resting his fingers lightly on the back of her hand. Sam was acutely aware of the single point of contact between them.

"Anyway, I got adopted almost immediately. My parents - my adoptive parents' - house is the one I did show you. Good people. Best thing that could have happened to me was that my birth parents were so crappy, so I could find my real parents. When they died I figured I had a choice. I could fall into the hole they left in my heart, or I could keep laughing." He squeezed her hand. She squeezed back, sympathetically.

"Because the thing about hurting is that even when it feels like it'll kill you, it really can't. It just hurts. And if the choice is helping it hurt, or finding the joy everywhere you can, I pick that one."

Sam narrowed her eyes. *So I'm doing it wrong?* She was affronted, but he also made a lot of sense. His smooth voice wasn't accusing, either. He understood how she felt.

"And when I saw you, babe, I thought 'that girl looks like joy to me' and I had to talk to you. You know what I like about you?"

Sam shook her head, "If you say it's my tits, I will kill you."

He laughed out loud, with his head tossed back and his shoulders shaking. "Well, they are fabulous. What I like about you is that I can tell you're like me. Remember when I found you and you laughed? And before that, anyone can see you've got problems on your mind, but any little distraction and you come to life. You rise above naturally," he tapped her temple softly with two fingers. "Right up until you think too hard and pull yourself back down."

Sam blinked. Nobody had ever seen her as naturally cheerful before. "Smile!" had been the constant refrain she got from her mother as she grew up, right after, "Can't you be more like your sister?" Her sister smiled all the time.

She scrubbed away her tears, "Tom, I just-"

He held up an elegant, dirty hand, "Shush, tits. I will abide by whatever you decide. If you want to avoid me, I'll stay away. If you think we can just be friendly, that's cool." He leaned in close and kissed her temple, exactly where he'd just tapped her. "But I would be happiest to share as much with you as possible while we can."

He stood and dusted himself off. Black smudges showed where he'd cleaned his hands on his jeans earlier. "Come find me any time," he said, and walked towards the light of the courtyard.

Sam stared into the blackness for a moment, then jumped up and ran after him. "I'd like to be your friend," she burst out when she caught up.

Tom grinned. "All right, but don't expect me to stop checking you out."

Sam burst out laughing. *Oh, you idiot. It is a BAD idea to flirt with your friend. Don't get attached, remember?*

Chapter 8 -- Choices

By the time they finished packing up the meat, Sam was tired again. She was also frustrated from trying to stifle her reactions to Tom's flirting and teasing. Most of all she was sick of every one of Tom's work friends strolling by and making a joke about meat packers.

Tom had tried to escort her to her room, but she had refused and for just a second his cool facade broke and for just a moment she saw frustration and longing in his eyes. Then they were gone again and he quoted The Princess Bride, "As you wish."

Sam could see that moment as she stared into the darkness in her empty room. Somehow, seeing his hurt drew her to him even more. *If Tom had come up, I wouldn't feel this lonely now,* she thought, and then, *but would I feel lonelier later?* She took off her pants, rolled over and fell asleep.

In her dreams Tom was embracing her in the middle of the deserted street market. She tried to push him away, but he held her so firmly she couldn't squirm out of his arms. He gripped her so tightly she couldn't get a full breath. "Let me go!" she gasped and pounded on his chest.

He laughed at her, not kindly, but with a mocking edge. "Let's have some fun," he growled. His eyes raked over her like he owned her, and there was a sexual power in his voice that Sam could feel her body responding to. She struggled harder, to no effect.

He captured both her hands behind her back, with one hand. In the other appeared the razor knife he had used to fix the cables the day they'd met. He cut the straps of her tank top, deliberately letting her feel the blade but not cutting her skin. She shivered at the cool touch. When her straps were hanging free he pulled the tank down off her, leaving her in just her lacy bra and panties. These he cut as well. The way Sam's hands were pinned behind her caused her full, firm breasts to jut forward, almost proudly. She tried to pull away again, and her struggles shook them.

He captured her mouth with his. The kiss was violent; his tongue plundering her mouth and his teeth grating on hers. It sent a jolt through her and she moaned involuntarily. He took her breast in his big, rough hand and squeezed the aching flesh. Her body melted under his hand and she felt herself fall against him.

An eternity later he released her mouth, but not her body. She looked up at him. "I don't want to..." but she trailed off. *Don't want what? This, or giving this up?*

Tom stroked her nipple and she leaned into the sensation. "Yes you do," he answered. He took her mouth again, demandingly. Again, she couldn't resist the excitement she felt as his tongue probed hers. She pressed into him, slipping her tongue between his lips to turn the tables on him. He chuckled victoriously and suddenly released her hands to grip the back of her neck and press her harder against his lips.

His other hand caressed her lower back and buttocks. Then it slipped forward and his fingers slipped between her legs. She moaned and twitched under his hand, as intense pleasure licked out from her center.

As sometimes happens in dreams the scene shifted. Tom's clothes were gone, too, and he held her up in his arms. She wrapped her legs around his waist and drove him into her. His fingernails dug into her back as she took all of him inside her warmth. He guided her hips, sliding her up and down his shaft and she whimpered with pleasure at the heat and friction of him.

They moved furiously against each other, and every time their hips came together the ground shook beneath them.

Her breath was fast and ragged, and she could hear him panting against her ear as they came together with a frantic, desperate motion. Sam felt herself clamp around him as her pleasure rose inside her. The building shook as her pleasure mounted, electrifying her with every stroke he made within her. They climaxed exactly together. Sam screamed wordlessly as pleasure rocked through her, Tom bit her shoulder and exploded into her, his final jerking movements sending little shocks of feeling through her.

And that's when the building fell. They stood frozen, still joined together, as it crushed their bodies beneath tons of concrete and iron.

Sam woke up with a strangled scream. Morning light glowed through the curtains. She fumbled for her phone. It was a little after nine, *and holy shit! I have service!* Her battery life was in the red, though. She flipped a light switch experimentally, but there was still no power.

I'll have to make this call count, then. She dialed Uncle Ty. He'd have the most information and a plan to get her home, and he could pass on to Isa and her parents that she was all right. She really wanted a long talk with Isa, but it would have to wait.

She got Uncle Ty's voicemail. "What the hell, Uncle Ty! I'm in a disaster area and you shut off your phone? Whoever she is, I'm going to punch her in the face when I get home!" She stabbed the end call button. She fumed for a minute, then she giggled. *Whatever, I do what I want!* She dialed Isa's number. She knew the proper thing to do would be to call her folks, but they couldn't help her right now and wouldn't do her morale anywhere near the good that Isa would.

Isa picked up immediately and wasted almost a full minute of Sam's precious battery life whooping and screaming Sam's name into the phone. "Oh my god! Shut up!" Sam yelled back. She could feel her face split in a dopey smile.

"Sam! Holy crap we've been freaking out. Are you all right? What's going on? Are you safe?"

"I'm fine, just a bump on the head. And things are pretty bleak here but I'm safe, I think." *Safe and confused.* "I've only got a little battery, though. There's no power. Do you know if I can get home? Is the airport running?"

"I hear it's basically destroyed." Sam groaned and thunked her head against the wall. "Don't freak out, though," Isa went on, "Your uncle's on his way to get you. He got on a plane as soon as he could, but air traffic all around you has gone insane. He's flying to the closest open airport and then driving to you. But you should call him. When he left we had no idea if you were even alive. He's scared to death."

Sam thought about the voicemail she'd left. *Whoops! Well, he'll sure know I'm alive.* Knowing Uncle Ty was on his way pushed her past giddy and into the realm of pure elation. "I called him first and his phone's off. But I should save battery so I can answer when he calls back."

"Hold on!" Isa went silent and Sam counted exactly 37 anxious seconds before she came back. "Looks like he'll be off the plane in about five hours. No idea how long it'll take him to get from there to you, though. Now, get off the line."

Sam could hear happy tears in her friend's voice. "Love you!" she said, and obeyed, feeling tears prick her own eyes. *I'm going to go home! Uncle Ty is on his way to get me!* She pressed the phone to her heart. All she had to do now was wait.

She opened the door to the hallway to go find Tom and tell him her news, but she hesitated and shut the door again. She felt so good right now. If she saw Tom the conflict between her desire for him and her decision to keep her distance would start to drag her down again, she knew it. The tension between them would knot her guts up in just a few minutes, let alone five hours. She'd been so unhappy for so long that she wanted to ride this joyful feeling as long as it would last.

Maybe I should just not see him again. He said I could. But then she'd have just disappeared without saying goodbye, or thanking him again for rescuing her. It also meant spending more than five hours alone, just waiting. She wanted to celebrate her good news. Specifically, she wanted to share her news with him. She knew he'd be happy for her.

So...what? My choices are be miserable or be miserable? She bit her lip. Tom had talked about choices. *He'd want me to make a choice that brought me joy, like he does. But I don't know if I can be like him.* She definitely had a lot more practice at being generally dissatisfied.

She drummed her fingers on the bedside table, leaving dots in the plaster dust the earthquake had covered the entire room in. *Can I just decide to not be sad when it's time to leave him? Does it matter? If I could go right now I'd already be sad to leave him.*

She looked at the phone still clutched in her hand. She had five hours until Uncle Ty called her. She could spend those five hours being unhappy, or she could spend them in a better way. *I spend so much time being overwhelmed, or seduced, or swept off my feet or just carried away. Screw it. I think I need to start choosing. I don't know if I can be like him all the time, but I want to be. And I can start by making us both happy for five hours.* Sam stood up. She only had a little while left here, she wanted to spend as much of it with Tom as she could, and not platonically.

Chapter 9 -- And the winner is...?

She searched the hotel from top to bottom but Tom was nowhere to be found. She was acutely aware of the passing time as she prowled the roof, the hallways, the conference rooms and the now deserted kitchen area. Finally in the courtyard she recognized an older, square jawed man leaning against the wall and smoking. He had enthusiastically supplied the most meat-packing jokes last night and seemed to be a friend of Tom's. *Of course,* she thought with a little shake of her head, *everybody seems to be a friend of his.* She might laugh at it, but at the same time she had to admit there were much worse things than that.

She approached the man, whose name she had forgotten if, indeed, she'd ever gotten it to start with, and smiled. His gaze slid right past her, his body language clearly saying, "You are no part of my smoke break."

"Hey," Sam said, "It's me. You know...the girl who was with Tom last night? I was really stuffing it in there, you said." *I can't believe I'm saying this.*

It was worth the awkwardness, though. His barking laughter echoed around the courtyard and he actually looked at Sam, rather than around or through her. "The meat girl! Yes, I remember you, meat girl." He grinned toothily.

Sam's normal reaction would have been to blush, or maybe say something nasty and definitely walk away but she simply didn't have time. *And I'm turning over a new friggin' leaf anyway.*

So she returned the grin and plowed forward. "Listen, I have to find Tom and I've looked all over but he isn't anywhere. Do you know where I can find him? It's kind of important." *Important to me, at least.*

"You are looking for Tom?"

"Yes. Quickly, I hope."

"You didn't pack enough meat yet, eh?" He wrapped his arm around his belly, apparently injuring himself with his own humor.

Sam grimaced and then forced her face back into a smile. "Sure. Actually, yeah you're about right." And suddenly Sam caught the giggles, "I do need to pack more meat. Ha!" She leaned against the brick wall and guffawed. The smoking man laughed with her and they both cracked up. Sam laughed until it simply hurt to laugh any more.

Dashing the tears from her eyes she looked up at the man who seemed much less creepy and intimidating now. "So anyway," another burst of chuckles interrupted her, "Do you know where I can find him?"

"Tom went home meat-girl."

"It's Sam, please." She stuck out a hand and the smoking man took it.

"Tom went home. He was tired."

Sam felt crushed. *You moron. Did you think he lived at the hotel?* She sagged against the red brick wall.

The smoking man finished his cigarette in one long epic drag and crushed the butt under his boot. He sniffed and peered up at the sky. "He is probably sleeping. But f**k him. I will drive you there, meat-girl Sam. What am I going to do here? There is no work today!" It could have been a depressed or even an angry speech, but the man sounded honestly thrilled at the prospect. Sam shrugged inwardly as a meaty hand grabbed her upper arm and she was half dragged, half carried around the building to a powder blue Volvo.

The drive might have been awkward, but the man, whose name Sam still had not gotten him to divulge, bombarded her with inappropriate good humor the whole way. Also Sam was busy forcing herself not to check the time on her cell. She knew she needed to conserve battery, but that was the only thing keeping her from marking every passing minute.

Luckily, the drive was short. Sam tried to pay the man for his trouble, but he waved the bills away like they were flies. She thanked him, and tried to get his name one more time but he just laughed and pushed her out of the car. "Go, meat packing girl!"

So, with her bizarre chauffeur waving her on, Sam walked up to the front door and rang the bell. Tom's house was very small but well maintained, sandwiched between two small shops on a road so narrow and short it was basically a glorified alleyway. She heard a few thumps and scuffles inside and the door swung open.

Tom was wearing only a pair of boxers, his eyes were bleary and his hair stuck up at insane angles. Sam was struck with doubt that she'd overstepped her bounds. *What if he doesn't want me to be here? What if there's someone else here?* She just stared at him, unable to come up with words that would properly explain her sudden arrival on his doorstep.

She could see him slowly start to come awake, realize who she was and where they were. His eyes snapped to life and his wicked grin played across his lips. "Well hello there, gorgeous," he said. "What brings you here?"

Sam drank in the sight of that smile. She didn't know it, but a similar one was tugging at her own lips. "I don't want to be your friend, Tom," she said.

He snaked his arm under hers and around her back, swinging her across the threshold and kicking the door shut behind them. He smiled down on her like it was his birthday and she'd given him exactly the present he wanted. "Well, all right!" he said. Bending down, he brushed his lips against hers. The move was so gentle that they barely touched, but Sam was so focused on him that the contact was searing.

Sam assumed Tom's house had a bedroom, but she never saw it. She pulled him down onto the carpet where they stood, enjoying having the advantage his mostly unclothed state gave her. She kissed and nipped him from his neck to his navel. As she watched him become more and more aroused under her hands and mouth, she felt her own excitement rising to match. Hooking a finger into the elastic waist of his boxers, she tugged them down impatiently. She flicked her tongue against the base of his shaft and was gratified to see him shudder and feel his fingers tangle in her hair and grip fiercely.

She worked him with her mouth and tongue until he was rock hard and gasping for breath. Then he flipped her onto her back and with shaking hands pulled off her tank top and bra while she hurriedly removed her pants and underwear. He started to mimic her, starting to kiss her neck and work his way down. But the feel of his cock pressed against her was driving Sam mad, teasing her by being so near, and yet so far from where she needed it to be.

She brought his face to hers and kissed him, letting her tongue explore his mouth wantonly. When she broke away she gasped, "I want you to take me right now!"

He plunged his hot flesh into her and she bit her lip as she felt him fill her. She arched her back and wiggled her hips, grinding against him. He pulled her up so they were both sitting, her relying on his strong arms to keep her upright as they thrust together. Tom caressed her nipple with his tongue and moaned, leaning back against his arm so that the proud, firm mounds of her breasts came forward, presenting the pink, sensitive peaks to him. He suckled and caressed them as he continued to plunge into her, the rhythm of their lovemaking growing faster.

Sam met his every thrust hard, each one causing a pulse of hot pleasure that hit her in the very center of her being. There was no place else she wanted to be at this moment but here, joined with this man. That she knew it wouldn't last only made her want him more, and made every white hot sensation that raced across her nerves more sweet. She cupped his face in her hand and gasped, "Tom!" as his pounding shook her.

He lay her back down on the rough carpet. She was so captivated by his huge dark eyes that when his fingers slipped into her wetness and began stroking her, her cry was as much surprise as pleasure. Pleasure won out quickly, though. He worked her with his fingertips in time to each powerful thrust of his hips and she writhed beneath him. The pleasure was so intense she dug her nails into the carpet, feeling that if she didn't hold on to something she would fly apart.

Sam shut her eyes as the final moment of ecstasy claimed her. Her hips bucked wildly, she groaned as tides of sensation shook her to the core. Tom's thrusts came harder and harder as, spurred on by her climax, he pushed himself to the crest of his own pleasure. He slammed into her a final time, tossing back his head and groaning. A great, shuddering spasm shook him and he exploded inside her.

They lay on the floor catching their breath and feeling the last shivers and twitches as their bodies calmed. Sam rested her head on Tom's chest and listened to his heartbeat. Sam felt more secure than she had in forever. Tom was right here for her, Isa was waiting for her at home, and Uncle Ty was coming from halfway around the planet to come get her.

She pressed her body close to his and told him about her phone calls and imminent rescue. If he was sorry at all it was buried under genuine happiness for her. He scooped Sam up in his arms, ruffled her already messed hair and kissed her nose. "That's fantastic news! I'm relieved for you, the waiting and no contact must have been rough for you."

"Actually, I was pretty distracted most of the time. I spent a lot of time with this guy who made me pretty happy."

"I'll kill him!" Sam laughed and punched his arm. He caught her wrist, using it to pull her in for a kiss. "So when does this rescue happen?"

Sam glanced at the wall clock. There was a crack across the face but it was ticking blithely away. She'd lost a lot of time in the search, it was now almost one. She had talked to Isa around nine. "Uncle Ty's plane should be landing in about an hour, and he'll probably call me then. After that it'll be however long it takes him to get here."

Tom stared at the ceiling without really seeing it. "He'll probably be coming in from Macau. It's on the other side of the Pearl River, across from Hong Kong. I hear it's open. If the ferry is running it takes about an hour and a half. If not he could rent a boat and be here sooner. Anyway," he straddled her and nibbled her neck, "We've still got some time."

They made love again, greedily taking as much joy in each other as they could while time allowed.

Chapter 10 -- Moving on

"So Uncle Ty called basically *right after* that. And Tom was super exhausted but he walked me back to the hotel. I told him about home, and you, and he says you sound hot." Sam took satisfaction in seeing Isa be the embarrassed one for once.

After an emotional reunion with her uncle, a grueling flight, and a full day of sleep Sam met Isa for lunch. Sam wanted to tell her friend everything that had happened, and Isa was happy to listen and make sure she was really as okay as she said she was.

Isa stammered, "You know I wouldn't try to take your - "

"It's fine," Sam smiled. "It was a one-time thing with us. We're going to keep in touch, but the magic's already gone." She thought for a minute. "Actually, you two would be really good together." Isa raised her hands in protest and Sam dropped that particular subject, though she didn't forget it. "Uncle Ty cried when he came to get me, but he'll tell you he didn't. And I cried a bit, too." She bit into her sandwich, to hide her eyes misting at the memory.

"Jeez, Sam. Things have been really weird for you lately. You need to take it easy for a bit, I think."

"Is this the same girl that dragged me to Yoga from Hell to get me out of the house?"

Isa stuck out her tongue, her go-to defense when she had no good answer. "Well that was before you added natural disasters to the list." She fake glared, trying to shift blame for a 9.0 earthquake onto Sam. "I'm just saying maybe you should stay in one spot so if another city gets destroyed it's only Buffalo. The world can stand to lose Buffalo."

Sam laughed. "Maybe you're right. I suppose I'd better crawl back into my cave." She pulled a brochure out of her purse and slid it towards Isa, whose eyes lit up when she saw the image on the front. "Racing horses across a seemingly endless wilderness isn't for me." She had most of the talking points of the pamphlet memorized, and so she went on as Isa flipped it open, her eyes getting bigger and bigger.

"Learning to barrel race, watching real rodeos, taking part in an actual fake cattle drive..." She gave a theatrical sigh and shrugged hugely, "Such is not for a disaster like me."

Isa threw a fry at her. 'Shut up woman! We're going!" Sam thought if Isa's eyes got any bigger they might explode. Only Isa's closest friends knew that her childhood bedroom had been full of horse figurines, horse books, horse pictures, and horse toys. Her apartment had what Sam called 'stealth ponies,' the figurines Isa could not bear to part with when she moved. She kept them hidden so guests wouldn't make fun of them. The first time Sam had opened Isa's closet to find a tiny plastic horse staring at her she'd laughed so hard her friend had to punch her to make her stop.

"We're going," Sam assured Isa, to keep her from getting absolutely hysterical. "I haven't booked yet but I want to go soon. Maybe the weekend after next?" Isa nearly fell out of her chair.

This already justifies the whole trip, Sam thought. She grinned as Isa tried to contain herself and failed. She squeaked like a little girl, "Eeee! This is going to be awesome!"

Sam nodded firmly. "We are going to have. So. Much. Fun."

...

Two weeks later, Sam was lying on her back, looking up at the emerging stars. She could hear Isa cooing to her horse off somewhere at the edge of the campground. Since they'd arrived, Isa had talked as much to the horses as to Sam. *It's just too freaking adorable.* She shifted, trying to find a position that kept the hard ground from aggravating her tired muscles and especially her aching bottom. *Who knew horses could hurt this much?* Despite the saddle sores and bruises, Sam felt quite satisfied, even proud. She was having an adventure because she'd decided to. She liked being the kind of person who went on adventures.

A mellow, masculine voice drawled her name and a second later a figure blocked her view of the stars. *He could have walked right out of a spaghetti western,* Sam thought. Their trail guide wore a button down shirt that had once been white but was now more dust colored than anything, tight fitting Wrangler jeans, chaps, cowboy boots, and an honest to goodness Stetson cowboy hat. His biceps pulled the rolled up sleeves tight as he offered Sam a hand and pulled her to her feet. "Y'all need to help pitch tents or I'm not feeding you. See if you can drag her away from those critters long enough to be useful." Sam nodded.

Smiling, she followed the sound of her friend's enraptured voice. Her hand tingled where his fingers had cradled hers and his thumb had grazed her knuckles.

THE END

Keep reading for a

Sneak Preview of

"COWBOY LOVE",

Book 3

in the

Samantha's

LOVE & ROMANCE

Series.

Denise Daniella Darcy

Sneak Preview of *COWBOY LOVE*, Book 3

Chapter 1 -- Welcome to the outdoors

This is perfect, like a dream, Sam thought. The morning sky was fluffy and pink, but the sun hadn't crested the tree line and the air was still a bit chilly. A small creek slashed and burbled and the smell of pine rode on the breeze. Jack's hands were warm on her skin as he unbuttoned her short sleeved blouse, baring her chest to the morning breezes. She shivered a little, but enjoyed the sensation when he unclasped her bra and stroked her bare skin. Sam had out of control brown curls and a body too curvy to be in style: wide hips and full breasts that she was still learning to not be self-conscious about.

They had grabbed a spare blanket when they stole away from the campsite and he lay her down on it, the fabric was rough on her bare back, but Sam didn't mind. She shimmied out her pants as he piled his own clothes and hat on the ground beside him. Sam watched the lean, well defined muscles bunch and relax as he moved.

He moves like a wild animal, she thought. He joined her on the blanket and she ran her hands up his arms, along his chest, and then behind him to grip his buttocks. The feel of the softer flesh over the hard muscle fascinated her.

He caught her lips with his mouth. Something about the way Jack kissed combined precision and passion in a way that overpowered her. By the time he released her, she was wriggling underneath him, her excitement making every nerve in her skin sensitive to the slightest puff of wind or touch of skin. When he stroked her she arched up to meet his hand and as his fingers slipped between her lower lips she clutched him tight and whimpered. He stroked and probed her, occasionally taking her mouth as well. Tingling heat and intense pleasure surged within her where he touched her. He slipped a finger inside her and stroked more firmly, watching her face as she teetered on the edge. "Oh god, Jack. Please!" she gasped. He increased the tempo and though she was trying to be quiet Sam cried out as waves of pleasure rocked her.

Jack picked her up and placed her on top of him. She slid down over his manhood, biting her lip to keep another moan from rising up. She rocked against him, the friction of their bodies moving together tantalized her sensitive flesh. Jack thrust into her as she rode him and every time they came together she felt another burst of excitement. They moved wildly together, the aching pleasure inside Sam building with every stroke.

When they were both gasping and trembling, Jack grabbed her hips. With no restraint he plunged into her, guiding her firmly down onto him at the same time as he abandoned himself to his passion. They climaxed together. Sam convulsed around him as he jerked and moaned, both of them senseless to everything but the white hot ecstasy they felt.

Sam collapsed onto the blanket next to him, trying to catch her breath and slow her racing heart. Jack cupped her breast in his hand and fondled it. She moved closer and fitted her body close to his. The cool breeze gusted along their skin, drying the beads of sweat.

Isa's voice echoed faintly from the distance. "Sam! Stop skipping all the work! Sam!"

Sam groaned. Jack grinned at her, the corners of his eyes crinkling, "Well, at least they let us finish before they got to hollering." He stood up and gave her a hand to her feet. "Come on and I'll make you breakfast."

Sam paused, one leg in her jeans. "You'll make all of us breakfast. It's your job."

Distracted by his shirt buttons, Jack just nodded. Sam laughed, "And now you're ignoring me, huh?" She scooped up his jeans, intending to lob them at him but his phone tumbled out of the pocket. She caught it mid-air, thought *damn, I'm good!* And then she saw the screen, lit up by her touch. And now the d*ream's over.*

She threw the phone at Jack's chest, where it hit with a smack. "Hey!" he looked up in time to see her dump his hat, jeans and boots in the stream as she stepped over it, still half-dressed herself, and stalked off.

Five days earlier...

Isa, Sam's best friend, sat on the other side of her desk. The vivacious blonde courier stopped by Morgan Advertising several times a week on business, and several more times a week just to hang out. The girls had been friends almost since the moment they met. Now, though she needed to get back to work, Sam was letting Isa chatter about their upcoming trip. Sam was excited too, and she wasn't looking forward to the tasks she had lined up once she finished lunch.

"I mean, I've ridden before," Isa's eyes were shining, "But only pony rides basically. I can't believe we can ride any time we want to for three days. Listen to this!" Isa pulled the ranch's pamphlet out of her pocket. In the two weeks since they had decided to visit the place, Isa had worn the paper thin from reading and re-reading. "Santa Monica dude ranch features riding instruction, three roofed riding arenas, and more than fifty riding trails."

"Well, it's a dude ranch. Riding horses is what we're paying for."

Isa ignored the sarcasm. "We have to buy cowgirl hats and boots. Have to."

Sam stayed quiet. They'd been over this already and Isa knew perfectly well that though Sam had allowed herself to be talked into the boots she absolutely drew the line at cowboy hats. *Nobody looks good in those things. I'll feel foolish enough in the boots.*

Stupid attire aside, though, the weekend could not come fast enough to suit her. *I just got back to work and I'm already burnt out.* She gave her computer a dirty look.

"Oh shit!" Isa glanced at the clock and jumped up like she'd been burned. "I have to go, I told Mrs. Spencer I'd walk her dog while she's gone." Mrs. Spencer was Isa's neighbor. Isa lived 15 minutes out of the city.

"Do you ever do any work when you're working?"

Isa turned innocent eyes on her, "Oh sure, tons. I am a slave to the vicious system of the courier industry. I'll meet you after you get done, okay?"

Sam nodded but Isa was already gone. She sighed and took as long as she possibly could to clean up their lunch mess, but even at a snail's pace the task only took a couple minutes. "Gah!" she mumbled and flopped into her chair. She had never hated the sight of mail in her inbox as much as she did now. "Gah..." she grumbled again and clicked the icon.

Sam,

Regarding your last correspondence I have to say I have never encountered such idiocy in any businessman. I must conclude that you are trying to ruin me. Billboards and radio ads are a step backwards that I will not tolerate, please generate a new six month outline. I will extend your deadline until Friday in the hopes that you can provide something less asinine.

Yours,

Jameson Kirkpatrick

"Gah..." Sam flipped her monitor the bird. She'd been practically running her Uncle Ty's advertising firm for almost a year now. He'd hired her out of high school and she'd risen from errand girl and coffee maker to junior partner with senior responsibilities. Morgan Advertising was the fastest growing advertising firm in the city thanks to Sam's hard work and crafty strategizing, *and I still make the damned coffee.*

And she knew that Jameson Kirkpatrick knew they were good, that's why he'd hired them. And despite his complaints and her own dearest wishes, she knew he wouldn't drop the contract. She just wished she knew what his problem was. And that bit about more idiotic than any businessman, *is that some sort of remark on my sex? What a punk!*

Kirkpatrick's manufacturing company made plastics products and had been very successful until several months ago when the main plant had been the site of an explosion that killed two workers and injured several more. Though investigations had shown the company to not be at fault, they lost appeal in the public eye and their buyers had been halving their orders, or even stopping them altogether. Her plan to rebrand the company and build a better public image wasn't anything unusual; a series of funny billboards followed by a run of well written radio ads. Only when those had reached a point of saturation would it be advisable to advertise on TV. No matter how good the TV commercial was, Sam was convinced if Kirkpatrick's got that kind of exposure before the mood of the public shifted then it would only come across as a tasteless move in the wake of a tragedy.

Sam gritted her teeth. If she let this man bully her into a bad campaign, it would reflect poorly on Morgan Advertising. *I've tweaked this three times. There's not much more room to change it around.* She wrote up a few variations on the original plan, and attached them to a response that she hoped was firm but not rude. *Well, not overtly rude, anyway.* "I would refer you to David Ogilvy before you continue to sneer at a proven strategy," she wrote. *Like this moron knows who Ogilvy is.* "Please select one of the attached or any of the previously submitted plans so that we can move forward." *Please select your ass and pull your head out of it.*

Get your own copy now of "COWBOY LOVE" to continue reading about Samantha's adventures in love.

Denise Daniella Darcy

Dear Reader,

We hope you enjoyed this adventure-in-love story.

Make sure you don't miss out on new and exciting stories by our romance writer Triple D. Join our Preferred Customer list to stay in touch. You will get:

1. *Advance notice of new stories in the series*
2. *Special deals for preferred customers only*
3. *Flash news*

Sign up now at:

http://www.denisedanielladarcy .com/newsletter

Cheers,

Sally Carruthers, *Triple D's Helper*

Rebound Love

Hi Readers, Denise here. I am busy writing more stories about Samantha's adventures in love so check my website **www.DeniseDaniellaDarcy.com** for the most up-to-date list. Happy reading! *DDD*

Rebound Love

Other Titles By Durango Publishing Corp.®

Denise Daniella Darcy

Recommended Reads

If you liked *FIRST LOVE*, check out these other great stories by popular authors.

Not Quite Dating (Not Quite series), Catherine Bybee

Tempting Her Best Friend (A What Happens in Vegas Novel), Gina Maxwell

Night Moves, Nora Roberts

Melt For Him (a Fighting Fire novel), Lauren Blakely

Midnight Betrayal, Melinda Leigh

About Denise Daniella Darcy

Denise Daniella Darcy, or Triple D as she is affectionately called by family, friends and fans, started life as a mortician's helper. Faced with the daily task of making the dead appear happy, she decided to switch careers and apply her talents to making the living happy instead. She achieves that through her Love & Romance novels. She writes from the heart, with a viewpoint that to grow you need to push your boundaries and you find happiness wherever it may appear and in any shape that it comes.

Triple D writes stimulating contemporary romances with passion, humor and a down to earth feel that resonates with her readers. She creates the 'I can't put the book down, just 1 more page before I turn out the lights' stories that keep you interested, engaged and involved.

Denise Daniella Darcy

Denise lives a vibrant and enthusiastic life on the west coast with a full house, including her children, cats and dogs, assorted critters, and her own personal hunk of a husband. The coffee is always on, the table always full of family and friends, and a spirited discussion is underway. And when evening rolls around, often enough a party is sent out to raid the wine cellar. Lively, fun and full of life.

Her novels include FIRST LOVE, REBOUND LOVE, COWBOY LOVE and CASUAL LOVE. This fall Triple D is releasing a new series in the young adult and teen romance genre.

To receive an email when Triple D releases a new novel, get on our newsletter at:
http://www.denisedanielladarcy.com/newsletter

And I know she'd love you to visit her at www.DeniseDaniellaDarcy.com.

Dear Reader,

One final note. Thank you so much for reading this story. I hope you really liked it.

As you probably know, many people look at the reviews on Amazon before they decide to purchase a book.

If you liked the book, could you please take a minute to leave a 4 or 5 star review with your feedback?

You can do that right here at: www.amazon.com/Rebound-Love-Samanthas-Romance-romance-ebook/dp/B00OBJ46QU/

60 seconds is all I am asking you for, and it would mean the world to me. Your friendly help will certainly help me in further research & writing.

Thank you so much, and here's to happy reading.

Triple D

Denise Daniella Darcy

PS. *Don't forget to get your*
FREE ALTERNATE ENDINGS
here:

http://www.denisedanielladarcy.com/
reboundlovealternateendings

Just my way of giving you something extra and thanking you for reading my books.